A Giant First-Start Reader

This easy reader contains only 50 different words,
repeated often to help the young reader develop
word recognition and interest in reading.

Basic word list for *Santa's New Sled*

all	hops	oh
and	how	old
at	I	on
but	in	really
Christmas	into	Santa
does	is	Santa's
Eve	it	sled
far	lives	snow
fast	look	so
for	me	something
getting	near	that
go	need	the
goes	new	time
here	no	to
his	not	very
ho	now	where
hop		will

Santa's New Sled

Written by Sharon Peters

Illustrated by Kathy McCarthy

Troll Associates

Library of Congress Cataloging in Publication Data

Peters, Sharon.
    Santa's new sled.

    Summary: Santa's old sled will not go on Christmas
Eve and he looks for something faster.
    [1. Santa Claus—Fiction.   2. Christmas stories]
I. McCarthy, Kathy.   II. Title.
PZ7.P44183San   [E]   81-5028
ISBN 0-89375-523-0   AACR2
ISBN 0-89375-524-9 (pbk.)

Here is where Santa lives.
Look at all the snow!

On Christmas Eve, Santa will hop into his sled.

Santa will go near and far in his sled.

"Ho, ho, ho! Look at all the snow!"

"Ho, ho, ho! It is time for me to go!"

Santa will go in his sled.

Santa will go near and far.

But Santa's sled is getting old.

Santa's sled is very old.

Now it is Christmas Eve!

Now it is time for Santa to go.

So Santa hops into his sled.

"Ho, ho, ho! Look at all the snow!"

"Now it is time for me to go, go, go!"

Santa goes near.

But Santa does not go far.

Santa's sled will not go, go, go.

His sled is very old.

"How will I go in all the snow?"

"I need something fast."

"I need something that will really go."

Santa's old sled will not go at all.

"Here is something fast."

FREE HELMET
WITH EACH
SNOWMOBILE

SALE

"Here is something that will *really* go!"

"Ho, ho, ho!"

"Look at all the snow!"

Look at Santa go, go, go!

3

Z P
Peters
Santa's new sled   889